The Crooked Angel

OTHER BOOKS BY JAMES KAVANAUGH

NON-FICTION

There's Two Of You
Man In Search of God
Journal of Renewal
A Modern Priest Looks At His Outdated Church
The Struggle Of the Unbeliever (Limited Edition)
The Birth of God
Between Man and Woman (co-authored)
Search: A Guide For Those Who Dare Ask Of Life Everything Good and Beautiful

POETRY

There Are Men Too Gentle To Live Among Wolves
Will You Be My Friend?
Faces In The City
America: A Ballad
The Crooked Angel (children's book)
Sunshine Days and Foggy Nights
Maybe If I Loved You More
Winter Has Lasted Too Long
Walk Easy On the Earth
Laughing Down Lonely Canyons
Today I Wondered About Love (Adaptation of: Will You Still Love Me?)
From Loneliness To Love
Tears and Laughter Of A Man's Soul

FICTION:

A Coward For Them All
The Celibates

ALLEGORY:

Celebrate the Sun: A Love Story
A Village Called Harmony — A Fable

The Crooked Angel

by

James Kavanaugh

Drawings by

Elaine Havelock

Stephen J. Nash Publishing
P.O. Box 2115
Highland Park, Illinois 60035

This book was written for my niece, Judy, who as a child,
had a physical handicap. The joyful energy and courage that
healed her condition then, still guides her journey today.

This book is lovingly dedicated to Judy,
the original crooked angel.

Once there was an angel

With a crooked little wing,

Who could only fly in circles

Like an angel on a string.

Because he had a crooked mouth

He couldn't even sing.

He only flew around and round

With his crooked little wing.

He had a crooked nose

And a funny crooked ear,

When the other angels spoke
He found it hard to hear.

The words all wer

n crooked

And they came out crooked too,

And even when he ate his lunch

He had a crooked chew.

He had a crooked eye

And a funny crooked jaw,

He got a crooked picture

Of anything he saw.

He had a crooked halo,

A crooked little walk,

No matter how he practiced

He had a crooked talk.

All the angel doctors

Just couldn't do a thing

To cure the crooked angel

With the crooked little wing.

No one seemed to love him

And his crooked little way,

He didn't have a single friend

To play like angels play.

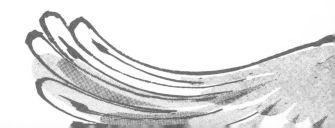

They flew away like flocks of birds

Whenever he came near,

He bowed his crooked little head

And shed a crooked tear.

His daddy told him not to cry

And tucked him in his bed,

His momma blew his crooked nose

And kissed his crooked head.

But nothing seemed to help him

To be happy and have fun,

Each night he saw a crooked moon,

Each day a crooked sun.

More and more he stayed inside
His crooked little room,
And shedding lots of crooked tears,
He filled the air with gloom.

One day he took a walk outside

When no one else was near

And thought he heard some crying

With his crooked little ear.

And when he got up closer

To the sad and lonely cry,

He saw a crooked angel

With his crooked little eye,

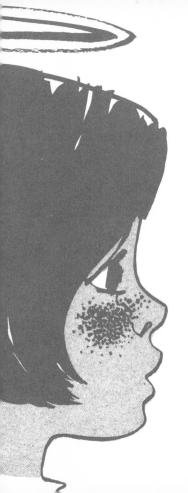

He walked a little closer

With his crooked little walk

And spoke as plainly as he could

In crooked angel talk:

"Why are you crying all alone?

"What makes you look so sad?

"Did someone have to spank you

"Because you acted bad?"

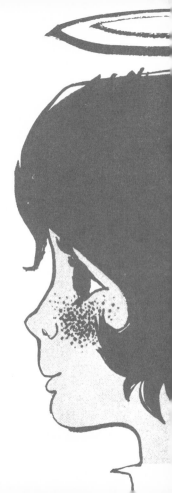

"Oh no!" the other angel said,

"I didn't do a thing,

"But I only fly in circles

"With my crooked little wing.

"EVERYTHING is crooked,

"My nose, my eye, my ear,

"And even when I try to cry,

"I cry a crooked tear.

"I just can't walk like angels walk,

"Or sing like angels sing.

"I just can't fly like angels

"With my crooked little wing."

"Oh, I'm so glad I found you!"

The crooked angel said.

"See my crooked little wing,

"My crooked little head?"

"I think you're very pretty,"

The other angel said.

"You've got a very pretty face,

"A very pretty head.

"Let's fly around in circles

"With our crooked little wings.

"Let's show the other angels

"How a crooked angel sings!"

Together then they sang a song,

And flapped their crooked wings,

They flew around in circles

Doing funny angel things.

They flew and flew and laughed so hard,

They rolled upon the ground,

Then they flapped their wings again

And flew around and around.

They laughed so hard they couldn't talk,

They laughed till it was late,

And when the moon came out that night,

They saw tha

t was straight!

No more they heard with crooked ears
Or saw with crooked eyes,
No more they shed their crooked tears

Or sighed their crooked sighs.
Next day they went to angel school
And played with everyone.

They didn't see a crooked moon.   Or see a crooked sun.

They learned to laugh with happiness

And each of them could tell,

That when they laughed just hard enough,

The world and all was well.

So take a trip to angel land
And visit them someday,

9 CLOUDS TO ANGEL LAND

Just find the two who laugh the most,

You'll know them right away.

They're bigger now and wiser,

They've grown and gained some weight,

But still they'll fly to tell you
How laughing made things straight!

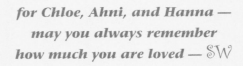

for Chloe, Ahni, and Hanna —
may you always remember
how much you are loved — SW

to my loving husband, Byrch,
and our wonderful sons,
Wyatt, Ryan, and Monty — YFR

text © 2009 Sandi Washburn
illustrations © 2009 Yvonne Fetig Roehler

Published by Growing Art Press
419 NW 16th Street, Corvallis, OR 97330
www.growingartpress.com

Publisher's Cataloging-in-Publication Data
Washburn, Sandi.

Good night, Grandma / by Sandi Washburn ; illustrated by Yvonne Fetig Roehler. – Corvallis, OR : Growing Art Press, 2009.

p. ; cm.

Summary: Written in a melodic tone, Good night, Grandma portrays the special and enduring bond between mother and child and poignantly illustrates how the power of music can help heal the deepest pain—the loss of a loved one.

ISBN: 978-1-934367-09-4

1. Grief—Juvenile fiction 2. Family—Juvenile Fiction. I. Title. II. Roehler, Yvonne Fetig

P27.W374 2008
[E] — dc22   2008933168

Project coordination by Jenkins Group, Inc
www.BookPublishing.com

Printed in Singapore
13 12 11 10 09 • 5 4 3 2 1

Good Night, Grandma

by Sandi Washburn

illustrated by Yvonne Fetig Roehler

Growing Art Press
Corvallis, Oregon

"Time for your bedtime story, girls."

The triplets left their toys on the floor and hurried to Chloe's bed. This was our favorite part of the day.

"Mommy, I miss Grandma," said Chloe.

"So do I, Sweetie. So do I," I said softly.

"Mommy, I miss her, too," added Ahni.

"Me too, Mommy. Will you tell us a story about Grandma before she died?" asked Hanna.

"Of course, girls. Let's see …"

I sat back in the comfortable overstuffed chair and thought about the many stories I could tell them about their grandma. My eyes lingered on the picture above the girls' heads, and I knew which story I would tell.

"When your oldest cousin was little," I began, "not quite as old as you are now, Grandma would babysit. One afternoon around naptime, as Grandma and Cody sat together in her big, comfortable chair, Cody asked her to sing him 'The Elephant Song.' She lulled him to sleep like this."

One elephant went out to play

out on a spider's web one day.

He had such enormous fun;

He called for another elephant to come.

4

"What about Tanner?" asked Ahni.

"Well, whenever your cousin Tanner scraped his knee or bumped his head or hurt his pride ...

5

"Grandma would hold him and sing to him to help him feel better," I answered.

"Did she sing him 'The Elephant Song'?" Hanna asked.

"Yes, Honey, it was 'The Elephant Song.'"

Two elephants went out to play

out on a spider's web one day.

They had such enormous fun;

They called for another elephant to come.

6

"What about us, Mommy? What about us?" asked Chloe, not to be left out.

"Well, when you three were born, Grandma would come over every day to see you. If you needed to be soothed or comforted, Grandma would hold each one of you and sing," I told them.

"'The Elephant Song'?" they all asked in unison.

"Yes," I said, smiling at the thought.

"'The Elephant Song.'"

Three elephants went out to play

out on a spider's web one day.

They had such enormous fun;

They called for another elephant to come.

"You loved that song. Sometimes Grandma and I sang it together, and we always sang in harmony. It made us all feel better." I sighed, wistful for that peaceful feeling of singing together.

"And sometimes we sang that song to Grandma," Chloe remembered.

"Yeah, when she was sleepy from her medicine," said Hanna.

"And when she hurt from the cancer," added Ahni.

WE LOVE YOU
GRANDMA

"Yes, you helped Grandma through her illness with your singing," I agreed.

Four elephants went out to play

out on a spider's web one day.

They had such enormous fun;

They called for another elephant to come.

"The morning Grandma died, you and Aunt Laurie sang to her, right, Mom?" asked Chloe.

"Yes, we did, Sweetie," I whispered, holding back tears.

"'The Elephant Song,'" Ahni said, looking down at her hands.

"Yes. Grandma's song," I said,

reaching out to hold Ahni's hand.

"I'll bet it helped her feel better," Hanna offered quietly.

"I hope so, Baby. I hope so."

1
2
3
4
5

Five elephants went out to play

out on a spider's web one day.

They had such enormous fun;

They called for another elephant to come.

12

"Mommy, do you think Grandma can hear us up in Heaven right now?" Hanna asked.

"I'm sure she can," I replied.

"Maybe if we all sing ..." said Hanna.

"She'll hear us, and maybe she'll sing with us ..." added Ahni.

"And then we'll all feel better!" said Chloe.

And we all sang a verse.

1
2
3
4
5
6

Six elephants went out to play

out on a spider's web one day.

They had such enormous fun;

They called for another elephant to come.

13

"That was beautiful, girls," I said, my heart full of gratitude. "Now, let's all get some rest."

"'Night, Mom. I love you."

"Sleep tight, Mommy."

"Good night, Mommy. Don't let the bedbugs bite," giggled Hanna.

"Good night, girls. I love you." I turned to leave the room humming softly.

As I pulled the door closed, Ahni reached toward the sky and whispered, "Good night, Grandma."

Seven elephants went out to play

out on a spider's web one day.

They had such enormous fun;

They called for another elephant to come.

Good Night